A Dog Day
for Susan

Written by Maureen Fergus

Illustrated by Monica Arnaldo

Owlkids Books

"Great-Aunt Alice is coming for a visit next weekend," said Spencer's mom. "She's bringing her dog, Susan."

"What's she like?" asked Spencer, who'd never met this great-aunt or her dog.

"She's dignified and graceful, with long, beautiful hair," replied his mom.

"I meant what's the dog like," said Spencer.

"I was describing the dog," said his mom.

After Spencer's mom went back into the house, Spencer and Barney stretched out in the warm sunshine for a little snooze.

"That dog Susan doesn't really sound like our kind of dog, does she, Barney?" Spencer asked.

"Woof!" said Barney.

"You're right!" said Spencer. "We *should* remember that underneath all that hair, Susan is probably just a regular dog."

All week, Spencer and Barney looked forward to having another dog to play with. Finally, just after lunch on Saturday, the doorbell rang.

Spencer and Barney rushed downstairs to meet their guests.

"Hello," said Great-Aunt Alice. "I'm Great-Aunt Alice, and this is Susan."

After saying hello to Great-Aunt Alice, Spencer tried to give Susan a hug. Barney tried to give her a welcoming butt sniff.

Susan sailed past them without a look, a lick, or even a tail wag.

Everyone followed Susan to the kitchen.

"What a lovely cake," said Great-Aunt Alice.

"I baked it just for you," said Spencer's mom.

"Thank you," said Great-Aunt Alice. "It will make the perfect snack."

Cutting a thick slice onto a china dinner plate, Great-Aunt Alice set the plate on the floor in front of Susan.

For a long moment, no one said anything.

Then Spencer said, "Can I have a piece of cake?"

"Not now," muttered his mom.

barney

When Susan was done licking the icing off her plate, Spencer's dad asked Great-Aunt Alice what she'd like to do that afternoon.

"Let's go to the zoo!" cried Spencer.

"Dogs aren't allowed to visit zoos," said Great-Aunt Alice stiffly. "Zoos treat dogs like second-class citizens."

"Oh," said Spencer. "Well, how about the beach?"

"The beach would be fine," said Great-Aunt Alice. "We can leave just as soon as Susan wakes up from her nap."

Susan slept all afternoon.

That evening, it was more of the same.

Before supper, Spencer missed watching his favorite show because Susan's favorite show was on.

At supper, Spencer's dad barbecued four juicy steaks, and Great-Aunt Alice fed Spencer's steak to Susan.

After supper, while Spencer was enjoying his cake,
Great-Aunt Alice handed him an umbrella and asked
him to take Susan outside to do her business.
Unfortunately, the umbrella wasn't for Spencer.

"It's not fair, Barney," Spencer grumbled as he climbed into bed that night. "Susan is treated better than me. It's like…it's like she's the human and I'm the dog!"

"Woof!" said Barney.

"You're right!" gasped Spencer. "Susan *doesn't* know what she's missing! We *should* teach her how to be a regular dog, Barney!"

Together, they came up with a plan.

The next morning, Spencer didn't complain when Susan got the last slice of bacon even though there was another dog and at least one human who wanted it, too.

Instead, he said, "Can Barney and I take Susan to the off-leash dog park?"

"Susan isn't the kind of dog who goes gallivanting all over the place," sniffed Great-Aunt Alice.

"Neither is Barney," said Spencer. "He just likes the park because it's a place where dogs are treated like first-class citizens."

"I'll fetch Susan's leash at once."

As soon as they were outside, Spencer said, "Okay, Barney, show Susan how to be a regular dog!"

Barney obeyed with breathtaking fervor. He strained against his leash. He barked at buses and cyclists and pedestrians and squirrels and fire hydrants. He gulped down stuff he found on the ground before Spencer was able to pry it out of his mouth. He peed *everywhere*.

"Are you getting all this, Susan?" asked Spencer.

When they got to the park, Spencer opened his knapsack and pulled out a blueberry muffin, a dog biscuit, and a wad of greasy paper towel.

Susan hesitated before helping herself to the paper towel.

"Good girl!" cried Spencer. "Dogs love people food, but they love garbage best of all!"

Susan's tail wagged just a little.

Next, Spencer pulled out his mom's hairbrush and started brushing Barney.

Susan watched Barney twist and squirm and snap at the hairbrush. Then, when Spencer pulled out his dad's toothbrush and tried to brush Susan's teeth, she bit down on the toothbrush and growled.

"Good girl!" cried Spencer. "Dogs hate getting their fur brushed, but they hate getting their teeth brushed worst of all!"

Susan's tail wagged a little harder.

Finally, Spencer said, "Susan, I'm going to take off your leash, and you're going to run away and not come until I've called you at least a bazillion times. Understand?"

Susan *seemed* to understand, so Spencer slowly unclipped her leash.

For one forever moment, Susan just looked at Spencer.

Then she barked in his face and started
chasing Barney.

"COME!" hollered Spencer. "SUSAN, COME!"

Susan ignored him completely.

Spencer, Barney, and Susan
stayed at the park for hours.

By the time they were ready to go home,
Susan was covered in burrs and her tail was
wagging so hard it nearly knocked Spencer over.

"You know what, Susan?" asked Spencer.

"Arf!" said Susan.

"You're right!" laughed Spencer.
"I *am* glad to know that underneath
all that hair, you're just a
regular dog!"

Sadly, Great-Aunt Alice was *not* glad to know that
Susan was just a regular dog.

"Where is her dignity?" cried Great-Aunt Alice.
"Where is her grace?"

"I think she left them at the dog park," said Spencer.

"And I think this visit is *over*!" said Great-Aunt Alice.

As soon as Great-Aunt Alice had packed the suitcases, she called for Susan. Susan came right away. She didn't twist, squirm, or snap as Great-Aunt Alice brushed her to a glossy shine and buckled her into the front seat of the car.

Spencer sighed. "You look just like your old self again, Susan. I guess you love Great-Aunt Alice even more than you love garbage, huh?"

In response, Susan gave Spencer a big, slobbery, garbage-smelling dog kiss. That was when he knew that she was going to be okay.

"Come again soon," said Spencer.
"Humph," said Great-Aunt Alice.
"Arf!" said Susan.

"You're right, Susan!" called Spencer as Great-Aunt Alice
began driving away. "We *will* be friends forever!"

For Sandy and Suzie, in honour of the millions of hours we've
sat around laughing at nothing and talking about everything. —MF

For everyone with a four-legged best friend. —MA

Text © 2016 Maureen Fergus
Illustrations © 2016 Monica Arnaldo

Owlkids Books acknowledges the financial support of the Canada Council for the Arts, the Ontario Arts Council,
the Government of Canada through the Canada Book Fund (CBF) and the Government of Ontario through the
Ontario Media Development Corporation's Book Initiative for our publishing activities.

Published in Canada by
Owlkids Books Inc.
10 Lower Spadina Avenue
Toronto, ON M5V 2Z2

Published in the United States by
Owlkids Books Inc.
1700 Fourth Street
Berkeley, CA 94710

Cataloguing data available from Library and Archives Canada

ISBN 978-1-77147-144-2

Library of Congress Control Number: 2015947567

The text is set in PMN Caecilia Roman.
Edited by: Jennifer Stokes
Designed by: Claudia Dávila

Manufactured in Shenzhen, China, in September 2015, by C&C Joint Printing Co.
Job #HP4309

A   B   C   D   E   F

Publisher of Chirp, chickaDEE and OWL
www.owlkidsbooks.com | Owlkids Books is a division of **Bayard** CANADA